KICK the COWBOY

By Joe Gribnau

Illustrated by Adrian Tans

PELICAN PUBLISHING COMPANY

GRETNA 2009

For Riley, may you never grow too old for stick horses

— J. G.

For Lina, my favorite and my best

— A. T.

*The word "Pelican" and the depiction of a pelican
are trademarks of Pelican Publishing Company, Inc.,
and are registered in the U.S. Patent and Trademark Office.*

Library of Congress Cataloging-in-Publication Data

Gribnau, Joe.
  Kick the cowboy / by Joe Gribnau ; illustrated by Adrian Tans.
      p. cm.
  Summary: A cowboy named Kick becomes a mean braggart, driving away all of his friends and terrorizing the people of his Texas town, until a no-nonsense little girl named Belle helps him to mend his ways.
  ISBN 978-1-58980-605-4 (hardcover : alk. paper) [1. Cowboys—Fiction. 2. Conduct of life—Fiction. 3. Texas—Fiction. 4. Tall tales.] I. Tans, Adrian, ill. II. Title.
  PZ7.G8777Kic 2009
  [E]—dc22
                        2009003950

Printed in Korea
Published by Pelican Publishing Company, Inc.
1000 Burmaster Street, Gretna, Louisiana 70053

The legend of Kick the Cowboy spread across Texas like a hot knife through butter. He wore a twenty-gallon hat, his belt buckle was darn near the size of Texas, and some said his handlebar mustache could stretch clear across the Rio Grande. Everything he did was better than all the other cowboys.

"Saw him rope a dozen longhorns in one loop," Clancy nodded.

"Heard he drove a thousand cows from Texas to Montana," added Charley.

"Yip, the greatest cowboy ever," said Slim. And the other cowboys agreed.

"The greatest cowboy," they smiled.

But as time passed, Kick acted as if he *was* better. The more he got above his raisin', the more he became downright mean.

"Maybe you boys should try workin' as hard as me," glared Kick. "Nobody ever drowned in his own sweat!" And each day Kick grew meaner.

"Just yesterday I saw him stare down a rattle-snake," Clancy nodded. "Snake never rattled again."

"Heard him growl at a coyote so cruelly the poor critter could only whimper," added Charley.

"Yip, sure is one mean cowboy," said Slim sadly. And the other cowboys agreed.

"One mean cowboy," they sighed.

Now Kick's *meanness* spread across Texas like a bad weed. Some claimed his snarl could take the curl out of a scorpion's tail. And for this reason, no one dared tell Kick about his horse. Truth be told, he didn't have a real horse. Kick rode a stick horse.

"Got me the fastest horse, right Clancy?"

"The fastest horse," Clancy nodded.

"Never lost a race, have I, Charley?" glared Kick.

"Not one," added Charley.

"I'd bet my bottom dollar it's the finest horse in Texas, right Slim?"

"Yip, the finest horse," said Slim. And the other cowboys agreed.

"The finest horse," they whispered.

Since Kick's meanness overshadowed his greatness, the cowboys found reasons not to be around.

"Say Clancy, how about we go to the waterin' hole tonight?"

"Sorry, Kick, I have an appointment," Clancy nodded.

"What do you say, Charley?"

"Sorry, Kick, I have a violin recital," added Charley.

"And what about you and the boys, Slim? Suppose you have dance practice," snarled Kick.

"Yip, as a matter of fact we do," said Slim. "Me and the boys are in the town musical." And the other cowboys agreed.

"The town musical," they shook.

"That's fine!" yelled Kick, and he hopped on his stick horse and rode away.

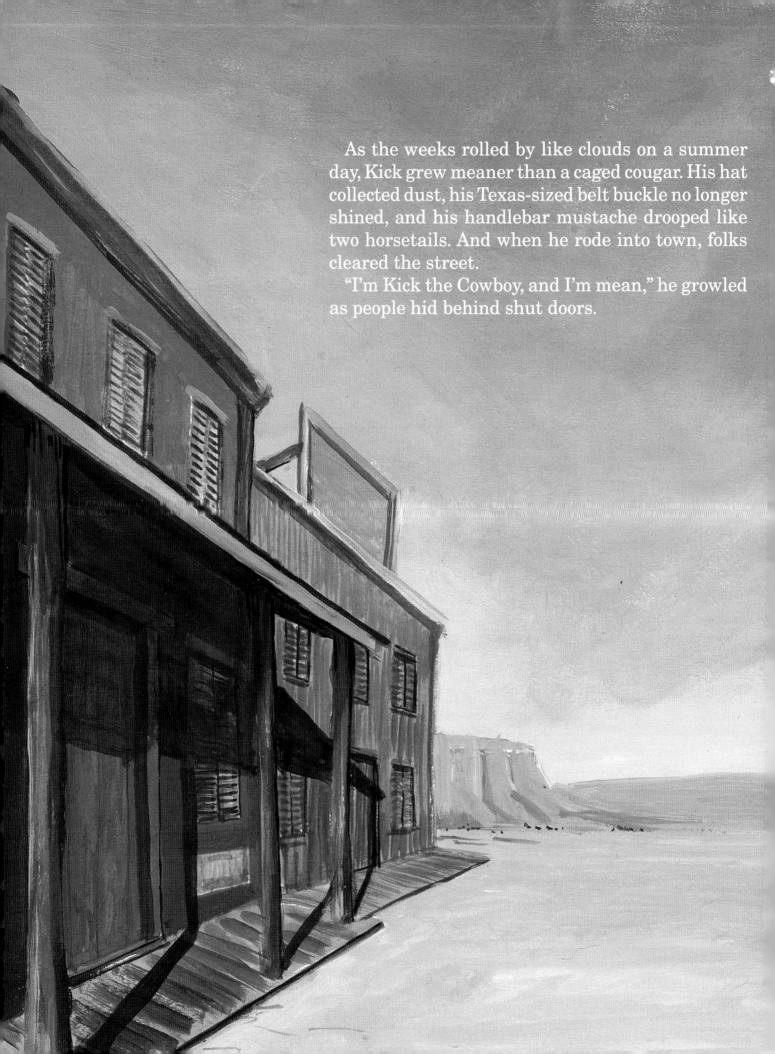

As the weeks rolled by like clouds on a summer day, Kick grew meaner than a caged cougar. His hat collected dust, his Texas-sized belt buckle no longer shined, and his handlebar mustache drooped like two horsetails. And when he rode into town, folks cleared the street.

"I'm Kick the Cowboy, and I'm mean," he growled as people hid behind shut doors.

But it was on this day that Kick the Cowboy changed.

Belle just moved to town, and during the night, her puppy, Poo, ran away. She looked everywhere for Poo. Her ma and pa were too busy to help, and her brother was nothin' short of ornery.

She was about to quit when she saw Kick. Belle didn't know Kick so she walked up and tapped him on the back.

"Excuse me," she said. "My name is Belle, and I can't find my puppy, Poo. I was wondering if you'd help."

Through open windows, gasps were heard as men cowered in corners and women covered their children's ears. Kick got off his stick horse, turned, and lowered his eyes until they rested on Belle. He squinted, snarled, and hissed, "Are you talkin' to me, little girl?"

Belle looked up and down the empty street. "I don't see anyone else mister, so I guess I am talkin' to you. I'm lookin' for my puppy, and I was wonderin' if you'd help."

"Little girl," growled Kick, "I eat puppies for breakfast!" Then he tipped back his head and laughed. And while Kick laughed, Belle did what no man alive ever dared do. She kicked him.

"Now why did you go and do that!" he yelped, hopping and holding his knee.

"Why are you so mean?" she yelled back. "You're just like my brother!"

"Why . . . I ought to," and she kicked him again, which brought him to the ground, eye-to-eye with Belle.

For a long Texas minute, they stared at each other until a single tear rolled down her cheek and plopped into the dust.

"Now, don't you go cryin' on me," he pleaded. "There's no need for that."

But Belle couldn't stop. Tears fell like fleas off a dog, and before Kick could say, "giddy up go," he was crying, too!

In the middle of Main Street, they cried for purt near an hour. And it was then he didn't want to be mean.

"I've been so mean lately I ain't got one friend, except for my horse."

"Now, don't be too hard on yourself," Belle told him. "Pa says that most folk are like barbed wire . . . they have their good points. I'm sure deep down you're nice."

"I know," he said, "it's just that I've treated the boys wrongly."

"When you're ridin' a high horse, there ain't no way to get off gracefully. You need to apologize. Life is like bustin' a bronc . . . you're gonna get thrown. The secret is to get back on."

"You're right, Belle," he sniffed.

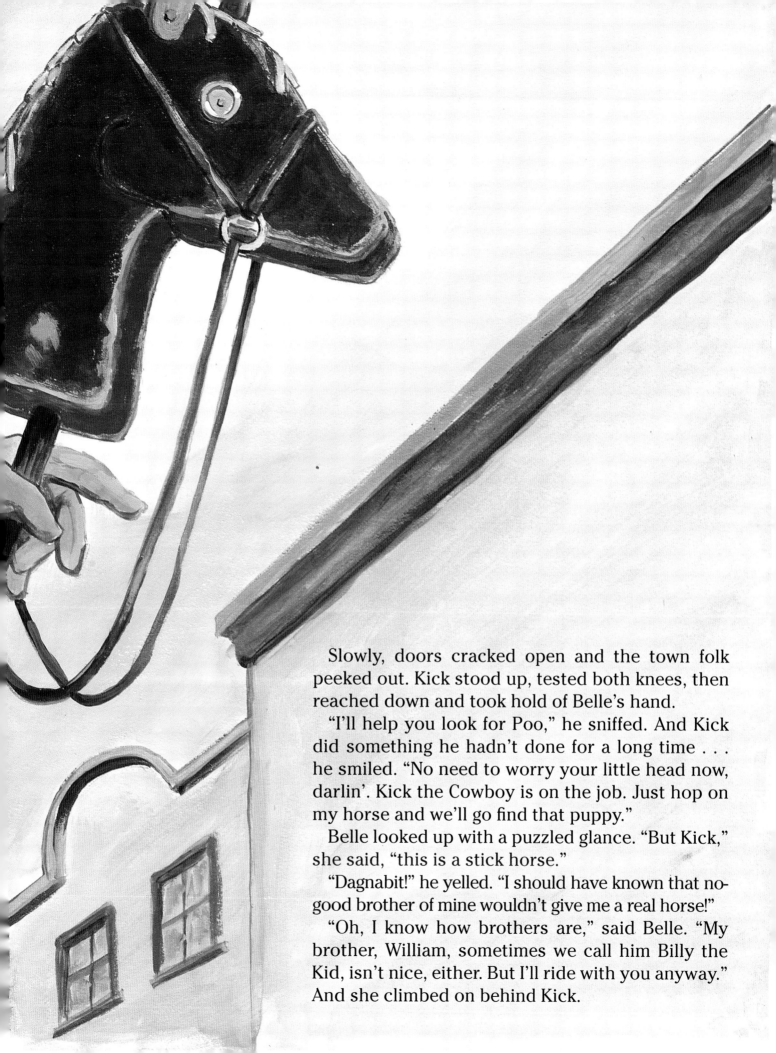

Slowly, doors cracked open and the town folk peeked out. Kick stood up, tested both knees, then reached down and took hold of Belle's hand.

"I'll help you look for Poo," he sniffed. And Kick did something he hadn't done for a long time . . . he smiled. "No need to worry your little head now, darlin'. Kick the Cowboy is on the job. Just hop on my horse and we'll go find that puppy."

Belle looked up with a puzzled glance. "But Kick," she said, "this is a stick horse."

"Dagnabit!" he yelled. "I should have known that no-good brother of mine wouldn't give me a real horse!"

"Oh, I know how brothers are," said Belle. "My brother, William, sometimes we call him Billy the Kid, isn't nice, either. But I'll ride with you anyway." And she climbed on behind Kick.

The next day Kick apologized.

"Never met a greater cowboy," Clancy nodded, watching Kick and Belle ride away . . . on stick horses nonetheless.

"Just today he helped an old lady cross the street," added Charley.

"Yip, never a greater cowboy," said Slim. "And you should see him dancin' in the musical." And the other cowboys agreed.

"Never a greater cowboy . . . or a better dancer," they smiled.